MIDNIGHT OF PLEASURE

39 Acrobatic Pleasure Zones

Mercy George

The contents of this book are strictly for adults

– 18 years and above

TABLE OF CONTENTS

INTRODUCTION

That sex shouldn't occasionally be sluggish, cuddly, unenergetic, or intimate is not at all what this work is trying to imply. It is a treat to be enjoyed; it does not need to be challenging every time. However, it is not necessary for it to always be elegant and romantic. When appropriate, sex should be intense, difficult, and mind-expanding. Sometimes having sex should be as intellectually stimulating as it is sexually exciting. Why not try one of these more acrobatic variations to spice things up? However, go cautiously, especially if you are not a very active person in general.

Therefore, nothing is more satisfying in those states than an acrobatic sex position that seems so enticingly unattainable that you can't help but feel drawn to try it.

I should make it apparent that the writer is neither flexible nor especially powerful. The majority of the physical sex positions on this list are too demanding for her to even think about attempting. She has aspirations, despite that. And if she can dream of completing a marathon despite never having raced a 2K or performing the splits while not being able to touch her toes, then she can fantasize of giving her boyfriend a blowjob while dangling upside down from his shoulders. Yes, that spot on the list is actually open.

While having sex is great, trying out new positions makes it even better. These stances are strongly advised for a variety of reasons. Learn about the various acrobatic sex positions in the next paragraphs, along with their advantages, and try out a few of them on your lover as often as you can.

Dare These 39 Acrobatic Penetration Pleasure Zones

1. X-RATED

The reason X-rated is so named is because your bodies resemble the letter X, providing the guy a very graphic look and allowing the woman to control the level of penetration. The man lays on his back, his legs outstretched and his knees lifted. Then she mounts him, riding him with her feet in front of his head and leaning back on her arms, and she begins pounding.

With the man's thighs encircling the woman and the woman's feet resting beneath the man's shoulders, angle your bodies so that you are partially on your sides to improve the depth of penetration. The man might then pull the woman onto him by encircling her hips with his hands. It is preferable to become acquainted to the basic posture and build up to this variant because it can be rather taxing, especially if the lady doesn't have strong upper-body muscles. The woman can increase penetration more easily if she sits straight up.

The Impacts:
This posture puts the woman in control and is ideal for the well-endowed male; the man would not be complaining, though, given the view he gets to enjoy. And even better, he may now freely caress the woman's thighs, clitoral

region, and chest with both of his hands.

2. FROGGIE POSE

By showing some Froggie style affection, you can make your vacation sea dip sexier. Start with standing sex with the male behind the woman facing the other direction. Next, the woman should slant her body forward and assume the breaststroke stance. When she is floating, the man should also assume the breaststroke position so that you can both swim into the pleasure zone at the same time. There is, of course, nothing stopping you from practicing this posture on the couch before you go. Try this in front crawl at a fast pace if you both have equivalent swimming abilities, but make sure you move together to avoid tipping each other over.

The Impacts:

As long as you are not too close to shore and you are both proficient swimmers seeking for a chance to enjoy private sex in the sea, you can't do better than this. Who, after all, would anticipate a couple to go swimming while having sex? Just make sure you both have good swimming confidence and can tread water before you attempt it. So that you can Froggie-pose grope each other.

3. THE SERPENT

When I claimed that the pose on this list that involved giving somebody blowjob while hanging upside down from their necks, I was not really lying. The Snake is without a doubt the most stunning interpretation of 69 that has ever been created.

The Impacts:

Fitness enthusiasts might find this entertaining to try. Large rewards follow: The blowjob is more exhilarating because of the blood rush to your brain during the posture.

4. BRACE AT THE BACK

The man is sprawled out at the end of the bed, his rod ready to go, and his legs elevated up into the air. Standing on the side of the bed with her back to the man, she slowly lowers herself onto his waiting organ. It's best to direct the woman with the man's hands on her hips while he finds the ideal angle in this deep-loving position. Once he has reached her, he can brace his legs on her back to force her to move forward and move deeper, or, if he is content with how she is positioned, he can let his feet splay on either side of her body. To prevent thrusting, the lady should elevate and lower herself using her leg muscles. The woman might lean forward to touch her toes, forcing his penis directly into her G-spot for intensely arousing sex. To prevent folding the man's penis at an unpleasant curve, move slowly though.

The Impacts:

This will assist you in building up to the Skier if you are drawn to it but lack the necessary thigh strength. If you happen to have a mirror nearby, talk about an attention seeker excitement: the woman is free to stroke her own torso as much as she likes. The woman can easily deploy her hands to provide the maximum pleasures if the man is interested in ball movement or backdoor fun. On a number of levels, this posture is advantageous.

5. THE ARCH

I can support the Arch primarily because the penetrating partner must perform the acrobatics. The only movement required of the receiver is a simple straddle and squat, which calls for some thigh energy but little mobility. Penetration may now be the most straightforward for certain people. Others will find it simpler to penetrate once the receptive spouse reclines and places their ankles on their partner's shoulders. The choice of what feels best for you and your lover is entirely up to you!

The Impact:
This position offers equal possibility for enjoyment for those who have both vaginas and prostates, as it angles penetrating in a way that is able to spur either the P-Spot for those who have prostates or the G-Spot for those who have vaginas.

6. DIVERGENT PERSONALITY

The man reclines against a couch, bed, or wall while seated on the floor. The lady then mounts him in a complete split as opposed to a sideways split, as with the Skewered Hurdler, leaning forward onto her hands to aid in the control of her motions. If he wants, he can put his hands on the woman's hips and waist to encourage her to move more forcefully. The guy can lift his legs high and bend forward to grab his ankles, which will boost stability and deeper penetration. He will be handing the woman complete control if he's in the mood to be subservient, which is just what the doctor intended.

The Impacts:

Would you like to experience the highest level of combined G-spot and clitoral thrills? If the lady is particularly ungracious, the gentleman can always use his hands to provide the main objective by letting them wander all over her body. Obviously, if he enjoys ball-spot spur, nothing can prohibit her from repaying the deal.

7. THE HILL

In the Hill, the penetrating partner enters them from a handstand position while the receiving partner merely stands against the wall. At this juncture, the receiver should likely intervene as a power bottom and control the thrusting scenario, but not too strongly lest they knock themselves down.   A   great respect should be given to the one on top if they can handstand while thrusting.

The Impacts:

When a partner approaches from behind, there is ample opportunity for them to use their hands or a toy to stimulate the receiving partner, enhancing enjoyment even when you just have a short amount of time. Looking at each other will make you feel incredibly connected to one another, and you'll also work out your triceps. Double success for G-spot or prostate stimulation, it works especially well.

8. THE ZOMBIE POSE

For those of us who can be flexible without going overboard, the zombie position is ideal. With your knees bowed, are you able to reach your toes conveniently? You can manage this. One partner sits on the floor as the other partner towers above them and stoops to one side in this folded variant of 69. The genitalia of the rising partner are in the spotlight for the seated partner, while the genitalia of the seated partner are in the spotlight for the rising partner. Everybody benefits.

9. THE STANDING SLIDE

The penetrating partner should move up against the wall so that only their head and shoulders are touching the floor, and then rest on the wall with the whole of their body as stable as possible. The other partner would engage them by facing themselves and coming as near as they can, roughly from the breast to the knee, based on height. When the recipient partner has reached their partner's penis or Velcro, they should open their legs slightly and crouch. After this, they have control over the penetration degree and rate. Imagine this as a greatly refined kind of reversed cowgirl.

The Impacts:

If you work from home and are required to sit before a keyboard all day, having a standing pose sex might be a game changer. You frequently develop a stiff neck from sitting slumped over a screen all day. The last element you need is to put pressure on the spinal cord or make your weary body worse when you regularly have sex while laying-down. You can try several sexual positions while standing that will engage your abdominal muscles and improve your vitality. A beam, a fence, a wall, or even a chair might be used as support. Standing sex provides you liberty and shakes up the routine of the bedroom. Anyplace can be a place for intimacy. Problems with laundering the sheets won't exist either. You don't even have to remove all of your clothing, in a strange sense.

Many couples do not consider having standing sex. Offer your lover this sex technique or posture if you would like to spice up your relationship and shake up the routine for them. To spice things up, try performing sex before a mirror. In this situation, intimacy is possible. As you will be in this posture, you will be more face to face than in other situations, which improves communication. Additionally, talking about standing sex with your spouse may simply fascinate them and, in some situations, spark arousal. Since it takes two to tango, both of you should be engaged in how it should be done.

10.   L FOR LOVE

Find interesting new methods to stretch your thigh muscles! The woman elevates her upper leg in the air while lying on her side and stabilizes it with her arm. Then he slides in while straddling her. This posture can be elevated to entirely new planes with a bullet vibrator. The male thrusts while the woman only holds the vibe against her clit. The woman's higher leg can be raised and rested against the man's chest if it becomes fatigued for a bit before returning to the original posture. This allows the lady to rest while also altering the angle of penetration, which alters the feeling. Who knows, you might arrive at locations you've never been before!

The Impacts:

When you're flexible enough to appreciate L Is for Loving, all those hours spent working out will have paid off. If the man is a leg man, he will be in ecstasy when he sees her beautiful limbs extended out in front of him. Both participants can effortlessly caress the woman's breasts or clit during sex.

11.   THE SUPERMAN

Superman needs both partners to have tremendous core strength. Imagine wrapping your legs around the body of your lover in a doggy-style position. But now they're standing, leaning back, and you are hovering in midair rather than them crouching and you lying forward. If penetration occurs before or after this posture is achieved is unknown, but either way, it is an extremely insane experience for everyone involved, most likely in a positive way.

It is strongly advised a sex swing for this posture if you are going a little daring! Almost all sex poses, particularly the superman, are made simpler and more enjoyable by a sex swing. The partner being penetrated can keep swinging although lying flat, and the thrusts from the partner over will be assisted by the swing's velocity. The swing takes care of everything, so you won't have to!

The Impact:

Do you enjoy the powerful thrusts and savage undertones of dog style? Okay, welcome to your new favorite job. In addition to being extra-pleasant for the male, the superman provides extensive entry to rub the super-sensitive area at the apex of her vagina.

12.   THE AQUARIUS POSE

If you are extremely good at bridges, perform one before letting your lover pierce you. As they do this, partially suspend yourself by wrapping your legs around their butt. They can certainly take the pounding from here, but if you want to truly show off your acrobatic skills, you might still step in as a power bottom.

13.   INCHES AND FEET

The slight gymnastics required in this posture call for regulated contraction of the pelvic floor muscles. The woman is on her bed, her head propped up on a cushion. With his legs at her shoulders and his head at her legs, the man is positioned on top of her. Using her pelvic floor muscles to assist her sustain the posture, the lady elevates her feet and bends her hips to enable the male to penetrate her. Once you are linked, contract your pelvic floor muscles simultaneously to excite one another in novel ways. While resting on her back, the lady can contract her pelvic floor muscles, which she can then use to slowly lift her pelvis while maintaining her hips and feet flat on the mattress. This guarantees a firm grip over the pelvic floor. The lady can gradually get out of bed as the guy thrusts, maintaining pelvic floor contraction for deeper penetration. Keep your breathing regular throughout. The man's tense muscles can make it more difficult for him to enter. If so, the woman may just lightly bear down with her vaginal muscles to facilitate entry.

The Impacts:

What more could you want for if he enjoys loving women's private parts? After all, everything is offered in a playable state. Additionally, all that exertion will keep your heart racing and heighten your passion as you approach the climax. Don't be shocked if female ejaculation occurs in this position due to the unique angle that forces the glans against the G-spot. Laying down a towel could be a nice idea.

14.   THE OLYMPUS POSE

The reality that the Olympus seems simple is evidence of how difficult every other posture on this list is. There are no walls to rest on, so wrap your legs around your lover and have them support you. Only use one arm to grasp on; let the other roam. This will make things more difficult. It makes no difference if you are in his arms for you to ascend to heaven or descend at an unlimited rate of speed. The male sex-skewers the woman on his penis as he picks her up. Female spouse's legs round his thighs on both sides, and he clutches her waistline with one hand while holding her buttocks with the other. In order to expose her eager yet uncaressed breast in front of the man's lips, the woman leans her head backward. She may clutch his neck and stroke the powerful man's back and chest with her hand held. As an option, practicing this posture next to a wall will make it simpler for the man to keep his female partner in place.

The Impacts:

This include greater penetration and activation of the G- and P-spots. Because both the male and the woman are engaged in activity, there is no place for breast kissing or caressing.

15.   THE CRADLE POSE

Sit your partner in a position similar to the butterfly stretch. Then, with your back to her and your legs bent, as if you were performing the child's posture to the air, get onto her lap and have her raise you up. Your partner may completely control the degree and intensity of penetration because you are completely limb-free, rendering you completely obedient.

The Impacts:

If done correctly, this low-intensity posture induces a great deal of personal touch and closeness as well as a slow build-up to orgasm. Although it's likely not the type to attempt on a first date, it can still be beneficial.

16.   **THE NO.14**

The stance of lovers in the song, where the male is No.14 and the woman is curled around him like a fourteen, gives rise to the song's title, NO. 14. The woman jumps up to lock her legs around the man's waist and hips and slides him inside of her as he gets up and get into stance. She then raises and lowers herself on him using the muscles in her pelvic floor. To add his unique beat, the guy tenses and relaxes his hip muscles. Attempt this posture with the female's buttocks lying on the edge of the bed if your level of ability may use some improvement. The original No. 14 still gives the thorough penetration and clitoral pleasure, but the man may need to stoop to get his pelvis parallel with hers.

The Impacts

The G-spot is hit? Awesome! clitoral sensation and pelvic rubbing that is incredibly sexy? Check! gives you plenty of room for hugs and kisses? Wow! You may say that this job fulfills all requirements. Each of you get a tremendous leg exercise from it, and all that clenching was well deserved. It boosts your final orgasmic outburst by pumping blood to your parts, making you more responsive.

17.   THE MERMAID A1

Have you ever bemoaned the lack of postures in which your spouse could pick you up and stab you from behind? You are totally comprehended by The Mermaid. Fold your arms and legs behind you, encircling the legs and arms of your spouse, respectively. Your spouse can then crouch down and slightly lean back, allowing you to swing off with them while they pierce you.

Even though it doesn't seem nearly as personal as putting your legs around someone face-to-face, it will undoubtedly feel more satisfying.

The Impacts:

Since your legs are up into the air, your vagina creates a tighter ring, giving a comfortable fit for his manhood and plenty of O-mazing contact for the two of you. This motion has these advantages. You can massage your clitoris or breasts while he observes you feeling yourself up since your hands are unrestrained. This will make him crazy. Switch from opening and closing your legs to adjust the stiffness and feeling. Do you want to alter it?

18.   MERMAID A2

Certainly, for experienced users only. You recline back into him as he is on his back and softly descend onto his genitals. Then slowly reposition yourself such that your back rests on his stomach area. Keeping your hands holding your legs steady, raise these into the air. So, he can stroke your breasts, clitoris, or butt with his fingers.

Why not practice yoga if this order to get relevant a flexible body? Additionally, a study published in The Journal of Sexual Medicine discovered that frequent yoga practitioners report overwhelming desire, arousal, orgasm, and general contentment.

19.   PERFECT BEE

In the concept of love, this posture is genuinely alphabetical. The lady sits atop of the man in a V formation, carefully angling her pelvis to aid the man hit her G-spot while the two people make a M shape. The guy may rest on a device to strike his P-zone if he is ready for anal play. Awesome! Begin with the male simply sitting as well as the woman in the traditional posture on top. The woman then balances by placing her legs over the man's shoulders and encircling his neck with her hands. If the man wants to avoid becoming entangled in his own limbs, he should just fall backwards on them after that. However, you might still have it.

The Impacts:

Due to the obvious angle of entrance and penetration depth in Perfect Bee, the G-spot is essentially impossible to miss. It is ideal for petite guys since it maximizes every available inch, giving you both more sensations. The guy's face will also light up at the nipple-tactic vision.

## 20.	THE WHEELBARROW

Do you recall the wheelbarrow of your childhood? No doubt, it has been given a sex-based twist by somebody. Simply enter the wheelbarrow posture, but rather than letting your spouse grip your legs, let him pull you closer, grasping your hip bones. It should make it simple for him to pierce you and manage the thrust's depth and pace. It need not entail letting them wheel you all around house in this posture as if you were using a wheelbarrow as usual.

The Impacts:

Clasping your hands firmly aids in maintaining balance. After that, he softly lifts and supports your legs as he penetrates you from behind. Why the female experiences it favorably: His penetration is satisfyingly profound. It is really a lot of fun. Why the male experiences it favorably, the pair can walk a lot in this posture, which is done on the floor, therefore its name - the wheelbarrow.

21.   PRIMA BALLERINA

The woman extends her leg into the air while leaning on a wall with her elbow extended. He supports her by gripping her leg while supporting her with his other hand, which he places on the base of the neck or hip to ensure her stability. Obviously, if the woman can easily maintain her upright position, his hand is free to move wherever else you like. A lady can perform it without using a wall for support if she is exceptionally balletic. But for an added challenge, the man can pull his spouse by the waist to have complete control over the gyrating. If you feel comfortable performing the master and slave role, this is fantastic.

The Impacts:

The male gets a tremendously sexy sight of his lover's buttocks and exposed thighs, and visual pleasure is a guaranteed method to make a guy rise up. The man's thickness will be highlighted and enhanced while the woman can take advantage of an uncommon posture. It provides the ideal amount of pleasure for both men and women.

22.   THE GOLDEN GATE BLOWJOB

Your spouse must lay back on the bed in the Golden Gate pose. To maintain his equilibrium, he must then stoop and place his feet on the bed. After that, you must kneel with your backside to your man's torso, exactly above his mouth. He may begin to lick you and do blowjobs on you. At this point, you must lean backward, exactly as you might in the acrobat posture.

You begin to offer him a blowjob as you bend backwards, keeping your knees on the bed, and arching your back to lower your head to the side towards his manhood. To stay upright, stretch your arms and putting your hands on the mattress. You are correct that this is all quite challenging.

The Impacts:

In the Golden Gate posture, all the woman needs to do is to maintain her awkward, arched posture whilst giving the male blowjobs on her. She must resist the need to smother her partner, which can be very challenging, in order to prevent him from unintentionally choking her.

In the Golden Gate posture, the dude's only responsibility is to devour her out. In this posture, he could feel like ramming into her mouth, but he does not need to. In event he suffocates or injures her unintentionally, he should just stand back and letting her do all the thrusting. Your partner can put his arms over your legs to assist in maintaining your equilibrium. But aside from that, he would not be doing anything else.

23. IN THE SKIER

The male is on the mattress with his rod poised to rock and roll, his butts near the edge of the cushion, and his legs up. Starting with her back on his chest and hips above his, the lady lays on top of the guy before sliding onto him. In order to avoid bending her guy wrongly, she must then gently sit up or move forward. She raises herself to a sitting position, gently places her feet on the ground, and then swings back and forth as requested. The male should maintain his lifted legs the entire time to make it simple for the woman to stretch between her own legs and massage the man's genitals and testicles. If that's too taxing on his knees, he can lean his legs towards her back. When beginning this posture, the female should lift herself using her pelvic muscles in the Pilates method. This will not only simplify matters but also stiffen things up.

The Impacts:

Although this challenging position might require women to have legs of steel, the Skier really is the best approach to obtain G-spot sensations because she may angle her partner in any direction she chooses. Additionally, she can restrict penetration levels if the man is a little too gifted.

24.   THE SWANS SPORTING

The Sporting of Swans can be enjoyed by everyone, however being physically active does assist. The man slumps to his knees and contracts his pelvic floor as he sits down. The woman climbs atop him, crossing one leg over his shoulder and placing the other over his flat foot for stability. Then, when the male flexes his pelvic floor muscles to thrust his member into her, she grinds herself to orgasmic bliss using her thigh and Kegel muscles. Wrapping her arms around the man's neck will help the woman balance more effortlessly. However, refrain from pulling on the neck as this could harm your back. She can be helped by the male placing his hand on her lower back or by him holding her bum; the latter action won't require much persuasion.

The Impacts

This is a romantic posture that's fantastic when you're feeling loved up since it allows for simple closeness and the possibility of eye contact and kissing. The man can stroke his partner's back as well; Tantric practitioners believe that this is where sexual strength lives. Not to mention, this is a clear winner because of the extensive clitoral stimulation.

25.   UP AND OVER

The woman slides onto the man while hooking her legs over his hips as he stands with his legs wide and feet separated by a few feet. She then raises her elbows and forearms to support herself as she leans back till her head rests on the ground. The man then thrusts while leaning forward until his hands and the ground are in contact. Assuming he is a gymnast prodigy, he can move into a handstand after touching his hands to the floor, but doing so will alter the angle making him seem much larger, so caution must be observed.

The Impacts:

This challenging posture will send you both into a tailspin as it requires adequate stability but rewards you with a depth of penetration, clitoral sensations for the woman, and lots of kissing. Certainly, there is also the sense of accomplishment when you maintain this stance without tripping.

26. THE BODY HUG POSE

The man is bending over the woman's body as she sleeps on her back with her legs hanging over the side of the bed. He is staying between her legs. She then stands up and utilizes his waist and shoulders to elevate and bring down her body for rocking while also wrapping her legs around his waist. When a woman is extremely flexible, she can try controlling the thrust only with her legs while still having free use of her hands.

The Impacts:

In this usually male-dominated position, a woman is in charge. The lady might feel more comfortable taking the lead more often if the man uses his free hands to examine her body. The woman will become more tense and tenser, increasing friction for both of you.

27.   THE HELICOPTER POSE

This sex position, which is by far the strangest one I've ever seen, leaves me virtually speechless. The penetrating partner hovers above them as the receiving partner gets down on her hands and knees, penetrating them from a hybrid plank/handstand pose. I'm not sure if the couples swivel their bodies to resemble a helicopter's movement, or if they remain still and simply thrust from this posture. In either case, you will work up a sweat since the job is equally crazy and fascinating.

Your bodies resemble the helicopter's blades, hence the name "helicopter," which you may have heard before. The receiving partner must assume the position of a downward dog, on all fours, with their bum tipped upward, in order for this to be effective.

The penetrating partner then positions themselves on all fours, but with their faces turned away as though they were getting ready for a 69. Swinging their leg over the receiver's body till they are straddling them, they should then insert their penis or dildo.

By this time, your limbs should be entangled, with your arms and legs appearing to be rotating like a helicopter's propellers. The receiving partner may either stay in downward dog at this point or, if it's more comfortable, lay flat.

The Impacts:

However, if you can handle it, it offers deep penetration and a distinct perspective to depart from the traditional missionary mindset. If you like it, of course, it is a fabulous experience. The helicopter position involves two people—a giver and a receiver—and is occasionally called the bumper car.

28.   PULL ME, PUSH ME

The Push Me, Pull Me is a more severe but slower version of Rock and Roll in which you both alternate between being erect and flat on your back, creating a wonderful variety of angles. Begin by sitting cross-legged with the guy within the lady, facing each other. Hold hands to help you stay balanced as you gently recline all the way back and then slowly sit up, moving your companion along with you. The feelings are strong and really arousing. If both of you have well developed pelvic floor muscles, do it without clutching hands together.

The Impacts:

Push Me, Pull Me is yet another tantric delight that offers a variety of angles, lots of eye contact, and passionate kissing. There is plenty of chances here to select the ideal angle that will satisfy you both. This position is all the evidence you will ever need that there is also a reason that Tantric sex has been known for hundreds of years.

29.   BOW AND ARCHER

It's time to extend those thighs out wide once more, but this time the woman can hold on to anything with her hands. She merely reclines on a bed or the floor, her legs spread as widely as possible, and her hands wrapped around her ankles. Talk about a free pass for the guy to crouch down between her thighs and start thrusting! The woman will have even more exquisite pleasure if the male caresses her thighs while he thrusts. The man can spread his thighs equally wide and lean in for a passionate kiss if he wants a true challenge. Yes, it's a stretch, but the clitoral stimulation it offers will be enough to satisfy him thanks to his partner's squeals.

The Impacts:

The day on which this posture was created, it is very possible that Cupid must have been thinking dirty things. The male has free entry to every part of the woman's body, watches every part as he will be eager to capture, which is certain to strike deeply into a woman's heart, soul, and pretty much everywhere else. Woo! In fact, you can even gaze tenderly into each other's eyes as well.

30.   THE BACKBREAKER

Only men with strong backs and good pelvic floor muscles should try this move. The lady jumps up and clutch her legs around the man's waist to penetrate while he stands. The lady falls backwards at   angle 90-degree   and he places   his   hands   behind   her buttocks and hips. She then rises to kiss   him   as he   assists her   with her pelvic   floor   muscles.   Repeat the leaning and rising to discover an astounding array of entry angles. Once you've settled on your preferred viewpoint, continue riding to the finish line! Just accelerate body movements faster to increase the toughness of this assignment.

The Impacts:

This posture facilitates a quick flow of blood to the woman's genitals even before kissing and caressing. By the time you begin to kiss her, there will be a lot of blood flow to her genitalia, simple touching of her thighs and buttocks, and more. The Backbreaker is a fantastic acrobatic yet romantic treat having amazing aesthetic appeal, no matter the form its name might evoke.

31. THE ROCKING HORSE POSE

Being flexible is essential for this twisted stance. Her legs are flipped over her shoulders to lay behind her head when she first lies over the side of the bed with her head resting on the mattress. The man enters the bed by sliding in while standing at the edge. After that, the woman takes her spouse's hands, they begin to rock while enjoying a deeper thrusting that is more satisfying than most others styles. The response would be a strong if the lady flexes her Kegel muscles while in this posture, close, and intensely loving moments.

The Impacts:

Rocking this way makes it possible for her to change the penetration angle in order to spur up her G-spot and or clits but much depends on her immediate desire. So, the pose gives her what she wants. No guy can reject such a posture.

32. THE SHY PERSON POSE

As the name implies, you support yourself against the wall while she raises her leg far away from the wall as she stands side by side with it. Then her spouse raises her lifted leg with his hand while standing in-between her thighs with his face to the wall. She is needed to be pressing against the wall, making the man's penetration deepens as he does the thrusting and rubbing his thigh against her clit. Leave the wall in case he wants a tougher challenge, let him support her torso with his hands only. Do not try this style if you have a poor back.

The Impacts:

A deepened penetration, abundant labial evocation, simple and free entry and eye contact are the effects. What kind of job could you possibly desire that is more adaptable? This position offers different sensation as the man Imagine how great it would be assuming the man is a genius with girth!

33.   TICKET IN FRONT ROW

Ready to be adaptable? This job will undoubtedly stretch you, so that's good. She reclines on her back with her knees resting near her ears as she raises her legs above her head. He squats on top, slides into her after she is sufficiently secure, he alternates between resting on her buttocks and bending forward to thrust inside her. If the lady finds it challenging to maintain this posture, she might support herself by lifting her hips with her hands. Additionally, it will be simpler to alter the entry angle as a result.

The Impacts:

He utilized to the fullest extent possible by this move. Additionally, it is wonderful for G-spot sensations and allows the woman simple entry to his perineum and balls. As the moment of climax draws close, he might lean forward, increasing the rate of penetration with his hands doing the pushing.

34. THE SKEWERED HURDLER POSE

The man supports himself on a couch or bed and rest his back on the floor. Then, in a sideways split, she mounts on him while her hands are resting on the ground so she can control how she bounces. In the event that she becomes fatigued, he comes to her aid by placing his hands on her hips to support her as she rises and falls. The extremely flexible chick may want to try leaning all the way forward so that her head rests against her ankle, giving her a continuous clitoral touch with the man's upper leg. If the man has the same range of motion as the woman, he can likewise perform the split, making it simple to get to his balls and buttocks.

The Impacts:

Although she is doing all the job in this scenario, she is rewarded handsomely since she is in charge of where she can simultaneously control the rate at which he thrust. She can also grind her clit against his leg for her pleasure. Since there is nothing else for him to do but to relax and watch, he will be free to hover around her breasts and any other parts he so desire. For guys just getting into their acrobatic sex routine, the Skewered Hurdler pose is fantastic.

35.   TOUCH AND DELIVER

This really beautiful position is not the sluggish persons. But if you are fit therefore, cross your fingers that you can recall those gym classes. She leans on her arms to support herself while she stands on her head with her knees flexed in front of her chest. In order to take leverage of her openness and vulnerability, he mounts her and faces away from her. In order to facilitate penetration if the angle is a bit too extreme, the man can lean forward onto his extended hands.

The Impacts:

Just say a burst of adrenaline! In case you flare for anal play, then there is ample space for your hands in this deep position but make sure you do well. He is expected to adjust his penis to fit in well with his hands because of how extreme the tilting is. But it would be easier for him if he is mounting appropriately on her thighs. To modify the angle and make things simpler, he should also gain support on the wall. To make things a lot simpler, let him stand before her, bend over then penetrate assuming she is the rigid type.

36.   SPLIT BANANAS

Do you have the impression that mastering splits is useless? The woman spreads her legs wide to leave herself open to proposals, and the man lies back and unwinds against a wall, a sofa, or a desk. Gripping her hips will enable him to assist her in pushing to and for as he likes to go further. Additionally, if the man is flexible, he may be able to split, which would place his balls in an ideal posture for a cool action.

The Impacts:

Although it might be a stretch, this open wide stance allows easy movement to every square inch of her rhythm, assisting him as his hands probe while penetrating her as deeply as possible. She can go all the way.

37.   A YIN AND A YANG

Unless it is currently positioned there, carry away your sofa from the wall to start. Make her balance her arms on the back of the sofa, then she headstands on the floor behind the sofa while supporting her chest on it. She then open wide her thighs for him to begin the action. He leans over her, made sure she is steady enough and raises his legs to press on the wall. This is dangerously amazing, ominous, and deep. Because of how many acrobatic postures a sofa facilitates, give preference to leather cushions or wipe-clean coverings. It's important to note that you should not try this position if you are not sure that the sofa is sturdy and hefty able to remain firm throughout action. She might even clutch her legs around her spouse if she is too acrobatic.

The Impact:

By employing this gymnastic posture, you can give a different definition to headstand. In addition to pushing deeply inside her, he might stroke her clit. This way they will instantly melt into one another when the woman's pelvic floor flexes and displays wantonly graphic imagery. Prepare yourself for an upheaval of your universe!

38. BENDING OVER BACKWARD

The time has come for the man to show off his back muscles. The woman now occupies a position of authority. On a couch or low bed, the man's bum is resting as he lays on the ground. She becomes a reverse cowgirl as she mounts and rocks herself to happiness. She bends forward and bearing her weight on her arms while she mutually stretches. She can also buck If she wants a G-spot stimulation. The greatest amount of pleasure is available through Bending Over Backward.

The Impacts:

In this posture, the man cannot help but declares clearly his wishes - he makes the most of his penis. He does all he can to keep up a proper body elevation from the floor, thus allowing his spouse the full charge. What else could a female do but board the vehicle and take off?

Is this work helpful? Kindly drop a positive review.

WARNING: *There are risks associated with every kind of acrobatic sex position. The composer of this work hereby calls to your mind that as you enjoy yourself also take note of your liability to these risks and be cautious. Otherwise, there might be some personal injury. Therefore, know your risk aversions, fitness as well as your ability.*